W9-CNC-174

Tick-Tock

James Dunbar

Carolrhoda Books, Inc./Minneapolis

This book is about something we cannot see, hear, touch, or smell. It is something we all have a sense of and we all have to live with. It is . . .

. . . so old it must have started before the world began. It has gone on ever since, right up until now. And it will probably keep on going, perhaps forever and ever. It is . . .

. . . something that can help us measure the speed of a
shooting star, or show us how slowly a snail crawls or a
plant grows. It also . . .

. . . helps us understand how long ago dinosaurs lived,
or how many days there are before our birthday. It is . . .

TIME.

Put your hand on your heart. Feel it beat, tick-tock, just like a clock. With every heartbeat, about a second passes.

Count your heartbeats . . . one, two, three, four, five. . . .

We can try measuring time in heartbeats.

What can happen in ten heartbeats?

In ten heartbeats, a snail can crawl across your hand.

Try standing on one leg for twenty heartbeats.

In twenty-five heartbeats, an ant can run across two pages.

For how many heartbeats can you balance a book on your head?

Your heart is always beating, tick-tock, tick-tock, and time is passing.

But there is a problem.

Your heart does not always beat at the same speed. It beats quickly when you run and slowly when you rest or sleep. So counting heartbeats is not an exact way to measure time.

This is an egg timer. The sand trickles from the top to the bottom in the time it takes to boil an egg.

Marks on a candle can measure time as the candle burns down.

A clock is our best way of measuring time. There are . . .

. . . clocks we carry with us . . . clocks to wake us up . . . clocks for lots of people to see.

Clocks measure time in seconds, minutes, and hours.

When a clock goes tick-tock, about one second of time has passed. We use seconds to measure time that passes quickly.

One second is about as long as a sneeze.

In fifteen seconds, a fly can beat its wings about five hundred times. How many times can you flap your arms up and down in that time?

An apple takes about two seconds to fall from a tree.

Flying fish can stay in the air for up to twenty seconds.

Thirty seconds to get completely washed and dressed seems like very little time.

In fifty seconds, a snail can crawl almost the length of one page.

Try staring into someone's eyes without blinking for forty seconds.

And still time goes on, tick-tock, tick-tock. Now sixty seconds have ticked away—that makes one minute. What can happen in one minute?

9

We use minutes to measure time that takes a little bit longer to pass. There is more time for things to happen in a minute than in a second.

If you talk for two minutes, you can say between two hundred and three hundred words.

It takes between four and five minutes to empty a bathtub full of water.

Now that you are getting better at measuring minutes, guess how many minutes it takes to . . .

. . . draw a picture of yourself.

. . . watch your favorite TV show.

Thirty minutes is about two thousand heartbeats, but who's counting?
How many different things can you do in fifty minutes?

When sixty minutes have ticked away, that makes one hour.

We use hours to measure even longer periods of time.

In one hour, most people can walk three or four miles.

Think of all the time you spend sitting down to eat.
It adds up to more than two hours each day.

In eighteen hours, a cat can drink about one pint of milk or water. An elephant can drink about forty gallons of water.

In twenty hours, some tropical grasses can grow ten inches.

When twenty-four hours have passed, that is one day.

13

There is enough time in one day to do many things.

In one day, we have daytime and nighttime. We also divide up the time in one day into morning, afternoon, evening, and night.

Night is for sleeping.

While we are asleep, time still ticks on. But in our sleep, we have no sense of time.

We seem to dream things in no time at all. We can fly to the moon and back . . . and we may be chased by monsters!

When we wake up, we have no idea how long we have been asleep. It is morning and another day begins. How do we keep track of the days?

15

The clock keeps on ticking, and time goes on day after day. To count the days, we look at a calendar. The calendar shows us there are seven days.

We do different things on each day. But there are some things we do every day.

Play with friends

Monday

Tuesday

Read a book

Wednesday

Watch television

Thursday

Friday

Go shopping

Make a mess

Saturday

Be happy

Sunday

Give someone a hug or feed a pet

Add these seven days together and we have one week.
Where does time go from here?

Weeks help us plan our time.
You can see the weeks on a calendar.
You can write down things you
want to remember.

Sunday
Monday
Tuesday
Wednesday
Thursday
Friday
Saturday

This Monday, I will go to Ellie's party.

Next week, on Thursday, I will make a robot.

Uncle Ben is visiting on Saturday in two weeks.

Three weeks is about as long as a housefly lives.

In four weeks, a human hair grows about a half inch.

When four weeks are put together, they make one month.

There are twelve months.

The calendar tells us the name of each month and the order they come in.

You can write on the calendar what is going to happen in each month.

January

February

March

April

May

June

July

When will you go on vacation?

In one month, you will have gone to bed and gotten up about thirty times.

August

September

October

November

December

Some months have festivals and celebrations when everyone has fun.

We put twelve months together and call them one year.

When twelve months have passed, the world is one year older. And your heart is still going tick-tock.

In one year there are . . .

about thirty-one million and five hundred thousand

seconds

which is about

five hundred and twenty-six thousand

minutes

days

three hundred and sixty-five

which is

which is about

hours

eight thousand and eight hundred

which is fifty-two

which is

twelve

weeks

months

which is

Imagine that when
the year is over
we could put all this time
into a big box.

one

year

We give each year a number. When one year ends, a new one begins. The new year will have the next number.

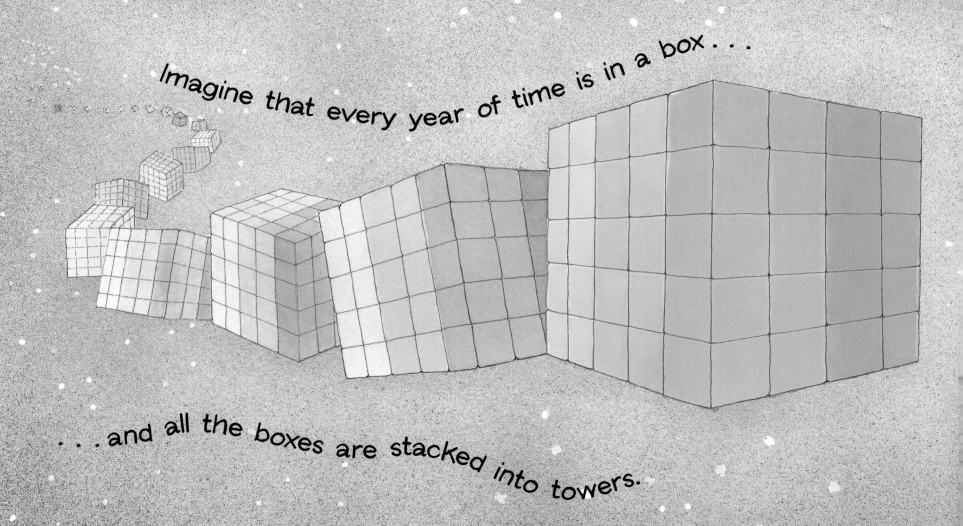

Imagine that every year of time is in a box . . . .

. . . and all the boxes are stacked into towers.

Ten years are called a decade.
One hundred years are called a century.

When a century has ended,
a new century begins.

SPRING

SUMMER

Over the time in a year, we see changes in the world around us.
These changes are called the seasons. Each year has four seasons.

26

AUTUMN

WINTER

When these four seasons are over, they begin again. And so the seasons go on year after year.

As time ticks on, year after year, everything gets older. But clocks and calendars cannot always tell us how old something is. Sometimes we have to use only our sense of time.

We can sense how old something is by how it changes over time.

six weeks

six months

two years

Sometimes we can guess how old a thing is by how it looks.

The time when there were dinosaurs on Earth has passed, millions of years ago.

The time when you were a baby passed a few years ago.

All this time is in the past.

The time when you will finish this book is coming soon.

Then there will be all the time that has not happened yet.

All this time is in the future.

As you hold this book,
read this page,
and look at the picture,
the time is now. . . .
And your heart is still going tick-tock.

31

Copyright © James Dunbar 1996

Published by arrangement with Franklin Watts,
The Watts Publishing Group, London, England.

This edition published in 1998 by Carolrhoda Books, Inc.

First published in 1996 by Franklin Watts, London.
All U.S. rights reserved. No part of this book may be reproduced, stored in a
retrieval system, or transmitted in any form or by any means, electronic,
mechanical, photocopying, recording, or otherwise, without the prior written
permission of Carolrhoda Books, Inc., except for the inclusion of brief
quotations in an acknowledged review.

Carolrhoda Books, Inc., c/o The Lerner Publishing Group
241 First Avenue North, Minneapolis, MN 55401 U.S.A.

Library of Congress Cataloging-in-Publication Data

Tick-tock / by James Dunbar.
       p.   cm.
    Summary: Introduces the concept of time and explains how it is measured in
seconds, minutes, hours, days, weeks, months, and years.
    ISBN 1-57505-251-2
    1. Time—Juvenile literature. 2. Time measurements—Juvenile literature.
[1. Time. 2. Time measurements.] I. Title.
QB209.5.D86 1998
529—dc21   97-14874

Printed in Singapore
Bound in the United States of America
1 2 3 4 5 6 – OS – 03 02 01 00 99 98